BUMBLE B

Mission FUN

written by
Marsha Qualey

illustrated by
Jessica Gibson

PICTURE WINDOW BOOKS
a capstone imprint

Bumble B. Mission Fun is published by
Picture Window Books, a Capstone imprint
1710 Roe Crest Drive
North Mankato, MN 56003
www.mycapstone.com

J QUALEY,
MARSHA

Library of Congress Cataloging-in-Publication data
is available on the Library of Congress website.

ISBN 978-1-68436-016-1

Summary: Beatrice "Bumble B." Flinn is funny
(she loves jokes), smart (she loves science), and creative
(she loves to draw). Beatrice is also very clumsy and tends to
bumble her way through life, which is how she got the nickname
Bumble B. (the fact that she loves bugs and hates her full
name plays a role as well). But clumsiness doesn't damper her
confidence! Every day she tackles a self-assigned mission. And
every mission is a new opportunity for success. With humor,
spunk, and a whole lot of spirit, Bumble B. proves, without
a doubt, that what doesn't kill her makes her stronger!

Designer: Aruna Rangarajan

Printed and bound in the USA.
557

TABLE OF CONTENTS

Meet
BEATRICE HONEY FLINN
(aka BUMBLE B.)

Hi, EveryOne!

I'm Beatrice Honey Flinn, but I prefer to be called Bumble B. You might think that is a strange name, but it makes a lot of sense. Let me explain:

1 My mom is a beekeeper, and my dad is an artist.

2 I tend to bumble a lot (which is a nice way of saying I'm a little clumsy).

3 My dad says I buzz through life with the persistence and confidence of a bee.

You mix all those reasons with a shortened version of Beatrice, and you get Bumble B. See? It all makes sense.

1 + 2 + 3 =
♥ BUMBLE B.

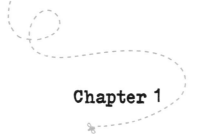

Chapter 1

SUPER COSTUME

"I have an announcement," Bumble B. said. "Are you listening?"

Her mom put down her coffee cup. "Of course," she said.

Her dad set down his book "Always," he said.

"I have a plan for my Halloween costume," Bumble B. said.

"Are you going to be a bee again?" her dad asked.

"Yes, but not just any bee. My mission is to make myself into a Super Bee!" she said as she held out her drawing.

"Well that's just perfect for my little Bumble B.," her mom said.

"It really is. Now, the cape is the most important thing," said Bumble B. "It has to be long so I can do this."

She whipped her arm in front of her face. She looked like a superhero.

"And I'll need a helmet," Bumble B. added. "I'll be buzzing fast through the air."

"I see," said her father as he looked at the drawing.

"Halloween is this Saturday," said her mom. "We don't have much time."

"Let mission super Halloween begin!" Bumble B. said.

They gathered two trash bags,
a bicycle helmet, foil, black tape,
yellow ribbon, and glue.

Bumble B.'s dad taped the
trash bags together for a cape.
Bumble B. and her mom made
foil antennae for the helmet.

Bumble B. measured and cut pieces of ribbon and tape. She put those on the cape. The tape was sticky. The glue was messy.

"I could use a little help here!" she said.

When they were done, Bumble B. ran to her room to put on the costume.

First, striped leggings. Next, her favorite yellow shirt. Finally, the cape and the helmet.

She raced back to her parents, holding the end of the cape over her face.

She opened her arms wide

and shouted, "I'm Super Bee!"

Chapter 2

SUPER BEE

Bumble B. and her parents rode their bicycles to the park. The neighborhood costume parade was about to start.

"Hurry! Hurry! Hurry!" Bumble B. said.

Her father tied her cape.

"I see my friends!" she shouted.

She started to run but tripped on

her long cape.

Bumble B. got up, grabbed her

cape, and tried again. This time

she made it without tripping.

"You all look amazing!"

Bumble B. said.

Rosa was a doctor. Kalia was
a dancer. Vincent was a fish.

"I see you are a bee — again,"
Rosa said.

"Wrong!" said Bumble B. She
whipped her cape up to her face.

"I'm Super Bee!"
Bumble B. said.

"A Super Bee? What's
your superpower?"
Vincent asked.

Bumble B. didn't
have an answer.

"Maybe you
make honey super
fast," Kalia said.

"Or maybe you sting extra
hard," Rosa said.

Bumble B. made a face. What
was her superpower?

The parade music began. Bumble B. let her cape drop to the ground. She started spinning and buzzing loudly.

Behind her, Rosa stepped on her cape. Bumble B. stumbled to her knees.

"I'm so sorry!" Rosa said.

"That's okay," Bumble B. said. "This isn't the first time my cape has been less than super."

"You're not a Super Bee. You're just regular old Bumble B. Flinn," Vincent said.

Bumble B. got up, dusted off her cape, and straightened her helmet.

"I'm anything but regular," she said. Then she held her head high as she joined the parade.

Chapter 3

SUPER CAPE

Even without a superpower, Bumble B. was ready to go trick-or-treating. Candy always makes her feel super.

She went with Rosa, Rosa's mom, and Rosa's twin sister and brother.

Rosa's mom asked, "What kind of bee are you this year?"

"I'm Super Bee," Bumble B. answered. "Let me show you."

She ran ahead, the cape flowing behind her. She made a quick turn to fly back to her friends. The cape got stuck on the neighbor's fence.

"I'm stuck! Help!" Bumble B. called out.

Rosa and

her mom

pulled the cape free.

"Why don't you just carry

the cape over your arm?" said

Rosa's mom

Bumble B. didn't feel super at

all. As they went house-to-house,

clouds rolled in. The sky got

darker and darker. Then came a

boom, a flash, and lots of rain.

"We need to get out of this rain," said Rosa's mom.

"Quick!" said Bumble B.
"Everyone under my cape."

Rosa, the twins, and
their mother got under
the cape.

"Good thing I have such
a big cape," Bumble B. said.
"Let's go!"

Thankfully they didn't
have to run far to get to
Bumble B.'s house.

"Anyone need a towel?"

asked her dad.

"We're actually pretty dry,"

said Rosa's mom.

"Bumble B. saved the day,"
Rosa said. "It was awesome!"

Bumble B. smiled as they all
got out of their costumes. She
would have to tell Vincent that
Super Bee did have a superpower.

Bumble B. was super at
helping her friends. And that
was the best power of all.

Mission

SCIENCE
CLUB

Chapter 1

THE FIRST DAY

Bumble B., Kalia, and Rosa were excited. Today was the first day of science club.

"Hi, Mr. Dan!" Bumble B. said. "I have the best idea for our first meeting. We can do hair science."

"What exactly is hair science?" Mr. Dan asked.

"We each rub a balloon on our head. Then our hair sticks up from the static. Hair science!" she said.

"I have something else planned for today," Mr. Dan said. "But I will keep it in mind for our next meeting."

"Okay," Bumble B. said. "What do you need help with?"

"We could use chairs at our table. We need nine," he said.

The friends worked fast.

"This is the last one!" Bumble B. called as she pushed the chair across the floor.

Bumble B. was pushing fast. She did not notice some food that had been dropped on the floor during lunch. Bumble B. slipped. The chair kept moving.

"Don't worry! I'm fine!" she shouted. "Just another bumble."

Bumble B. slid the last chair into place just in time. Other kids came in and sat down.

"We did that so fast," Bumble B. said to her friends. "We sure make a good team!"

They agreed. Then Mr. Dan
stood up.

"Hi, everyone," he said.
"Welcome to science club."

The kids all cheered. Mr. Dan
turned around to write on the board.

"Observation," he said. "Who
knows what that means?"

Bumble B. raised her hand,
but not as quickly as another girl.

The girl said, "It means looking carefully and noticing little details."

"Excellent answer," said Mr. Dan. "Observation is important in science."

Bumble B. was sad she didn't get to answer. But then Mr. Dan said they were doing an observation activity. And they were in teams!

Bumble B. and her friends

looked at each other and smiled.

They made the best team!

Chapter 2

A NEW TEAM

Mr. Dan said, "I want you to count off to make three groups."

Bumble B.'s heart sank. That meant she would not be on a team with her friends.

Bumble B. was with the girl who stole her answer and a quiet boy.

The girl was named Jasmine. The boy was named Otto. After they shared their names, no one said a thing.

Bumble B. thought, *I wish I was on a team with my friends. We would have tons to say to each other!*

Mr. Dan led the three groups out to the playground.

At least we are outside, Bumble B. thought.

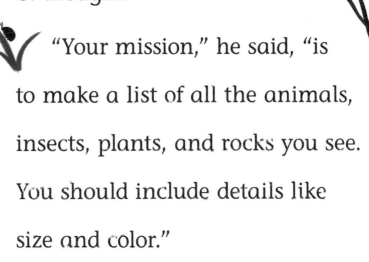 "Your mission," he said, "is to make a list of all the animals, insects, plants, and rocks you see. You should include details like size and color."

He handed a notebook and pencil to each team.

"I am a good writer," Jasmine said. She took the notebook and pencil.

"I am a good artist," said Bumble B. "I can add drawings to the list."

Otto said, "A list is made of words. It doesn't need drawings."

Jasmine nodded.

Bumble B. couldn't believe it! Didn't they know she was the best artist in school?

Mr. Dan told each team to

find a spot for their research.

Rosa's team raced to the kickball

field. Kalia's hurried to the school

garden.

Bumble B.'s team walked slowly to the playground.

"I don't see anything for our list," said Otto.

Bumble B. started to sit down on the edge of the sandbox. But she missed and fell backwards onto the sand. Jasmine laughed.

Otto said, "I guess that's why they call you Bumble B."

Bumble B. felt her face getting warm. Her hands formed fists, but as they did, she noticed the sand.

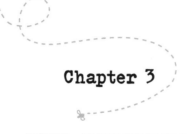

Chapter 3

THE BUMBLES

Bumble B. jumped up and brushed the sand off her pants.

"Sand is just tiny rocks. We can put sand on our list!" she said.

"We need details," said Otto.

They looked carefully. They saw that grains of sand were different sizes and colors.

Jasmine said, "Look! There's a butterfly by the fence."

They ran toward the butterfly. Otto tripped and fell on the grass. The butterfly disappeared.

"Are you okay?" Bumble B. asked Otto.

Otto said, "Yep. And now I am looking at the grass. Did you know each piece is shaped like the blade of a sword?"

"That is a good detail," said Bumble B.

Jasmine kneeled on the grass and bent her head very low.

"The grass is green on top but each piece turns white down by the dirt," she said.

She sat up. Otto and Bumble B.
laughed.

"You have dirt on your nose!"
said Bumble B.

Jasmine laughed too and rubbed her nose clean. Then she handed the notebook and pencil to Bumble B.

"Your turn," Jasmine said.

"I thought we didn't need pictures for a science list?" Bumble B. said.

"I was wrong," Otto said. "Pictures would be nice. You should draw a picture of the butterfly."

"Good idea. It was brown with white spots," Jasmine said.

"I'll add grass, too," Bumble B. said.

When Mr. Dan called everyone together, Bumble B. and her team had a long list of things they observed.

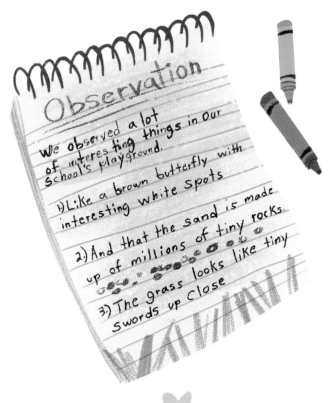

Observation

We observed a lot of interesting things in our school's playground.

1) Like a brown butterfly with interesting white spots

2) And that the sand is made up of millions of tiny rocks.

3) The grass looks like tiny swords up close

"I thought of a name for our team," Jasmine said.

"A team name? I didn't even think of that!" Bumble B. said.

"Well, you fell into the sand. Otto slipped on the grass. And I got dirt on my nose," she said.

Jasmine grabbed a marker. Then she wrote the name across the top of their list.

The Bumbles!

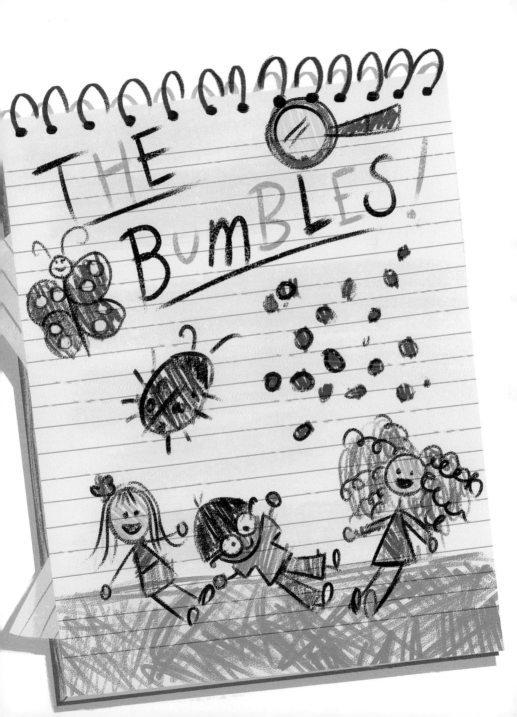

Otto stood up to read their list
to everyone. He showed everyone
the drawings as well. Bumble B.
smiled. She loved science club!

Mission

FARMERS' MARKET

Chapter 1

SWOOSH!

Bumble B. loved the farmers' market. She loved being outside. She loved helping her parents sell the honey from their honeybees.

She loved finding new things to eat. She loved dancing to the music in the market square.

Bumble B. especially loved visiting Kalia's family at their garden stand.

Kalia's grandmother tidied the vegetables on the table.

"Hi, Beatrice," she said. "And how are you today?"

Kalia's grandmother was the only one who called Bumble B. by her full name. Bumble B. new better than to argue with her.

"I'm great!" Bumble B. said.

"Kalia invited me to help make

flower bouquets."

"That's nice," Kalia's grandmother said. "Just make sure you get some work done."

"Don't you worry," Bumble B. said. "We are great workers!"

"Let's get started," Kalia said.

Grandmother's van was parked behind the stand. The van was filled with vegetables and flowers. The girls crawled in.

"Each bouquet has five flowers. We use rubber bands to hold the flower stems together. It's easy," Kalia said.

Bumble B. watched Kalia make a bouquet. It did look easy. She started one of her own.

Bumble B. picked five flowers.
She slipped a rubber band over
the fingers of her right hand.

Then Bumble B. slowly opened
her fingers. The rubber band
stretched into a circle. Bigger...
bigger... bigger...

Swoosh! The rubber band shot
off her hand.

Kalia laughed. "You will get the hang of it."

Bumble B. tried again and again and again.

"Or maybe you won't," Kalia said, still laughing.

Chapter 2

A NEW JOB

When Grandmother looked

into the van, she didn't see many

finished bouquets.

"You aren't getting much done. Go and get water for the flowers. I will finish the bouquets," Grandmother said.

On their way to the water faucet, they saw an artist making funny portraits. The portraits were called caricatures.

"We each have to get one!" Bumble B. said.

"The line is really long," Kalia said.

"It will be worth the wait," Bumble B. said. "Come on!"

When they returned with the fresh water, Grandmother had finished the bouquets.

She was putting them out to sell.

"What took you girls so long?" she asked.

"We got our pictures drawn," Bumble B. said.

"Aren't they funny?" Kalia asked.

"There is a time to work, and a time to play," Grandmother said, not smiling.

She took Kalia's water can. She filled the first flower bucket.

"I will fill the other one," said Bumble B.

She began pouring water. Just then, she smelled something wonderful. Donuts!

Bumble B. looked up to see a boy walking by with a bag of mini donuts. She wished she had some too.

"Bumble B.! Stop!" Kalia
shouted.

Bumble B. had watered
Grandmother's shoe.

"Oh no!" Bumble B. yelled.

Kalia just giggled.

Grandmother shook her head and took Bumble B.'s water can. She finished pouring the water.

"I sure make a lot of trouble," Bumble B. said.

Kalia hugged her. "You make a lot of fun!" she told her.

Chapter 3

BUCKETS

Once the bouquets were ready,

a customer reached in and grabbed

one right away.

"So beautiful," she said. "Where

is your garden?"

While Kalia talked to her,

Bumble B. studied the flowers.

They were beautiful, but
something was missing.

She whispered to her friend,
"I will be right back."

Bumble B. ran to the honey stand. She shouted hello to her mother and father.

She crawled under the table and grabbed her backpack. She found her markers.

Bumble B. ran as fast as she could back to the flower stand.

"Flowers need bugs," she told Kalia. She held up the markers. "Our mission is to draw them!"

"I was worried we weren't going to have time for a mission today," Kalia said.

"Don't be silly! There's always time for a mission," Bumble B. said.

They sat on the ground with the buckets. Bumble B. drew all of the shapes. Kalia colored in the details.

"What are you girls doing with the flowers?" Grandmother asked.

"We are making them better," Kalia said.

"You are drawing on my buckets?" Grandmother asked.

"It was my idea," Bumble B. said. "I'm sorry if I messed up again."

"We were just trying to help," Kalia said.

Grandmother looked at each drawing. Then she smiled.

"It's a great idea, Beatrice. Honeybees need flowers, and flowers need honeybees," Grandmother said.

She pulled money from her apron. "My hard workers should have a treat."

Bumble B. and Kalia thanked her, hugged her, and held hands as they raced away.

It just happened to be double-scoop
day at the ice cream truck.

GLOSSARY

announcement—an official statement

antennae—feelers on an insect's head

bouquet—a bunch of picked or cut flowers

bumble—to act or speak in a clumsy way

caricature—a funny drawing of someone

customer—a person who buys goods or services

details—small items

disappeared—to go out of sight

farmers' market—a place where people sell fresh produce, flowers, and other handmade items directly to customers

helmet—a hard hat that protects the head

mission—a special job or task

neighborhood—a small area in a town or city where people live

observation—act of noticing things

parade   a line of people, bands, cars, and floats that travels through a town; parades celebrate special events and holiday

research—a study to find and learn the facts

static—electrical charges in the air

stumbled—tripped

ABOUT THE AUTHOR

Marsha Qualey is the author of many books for readers young and old. When she's not writing, she likes to read, take walks by the river, ski in the winter, garden in the summer, and play with her cats all year 'round. Like Bumble B., she has very good friends who make life fun.

Marsha has four grown-up children and two grandchildren. She lives with her husband in Wisconsin.

ABOUT THE ILLUSTRATOR

Jessica Gibson is a freelance Illustrator based in Detroit, MI. She graduated from Wayne County Community College with an Associate of Art Degree in 2016.

With a pen and tablet by her side, Jessica loves creating adorable, whimsical, and quirky illustrations, ready to brighten everyone's hearts.